Lovingly,
Augusta.

[See page 1

THE YOUNG MAN HAD LEFT HER, SMILING, LOOKING BACK

JULIA BRIDE

BY
HENRY JAMES

ILLUSTRATED BY
W. T. SMEDLEY

NEW YORK AND LONDON
HARPER & BROTHERS PUBLISHERS
MCMIX

ILLUSTRATIONS

JULIA BRIDE

JULIA BRIDE

I

SHE had walked with her friend to the top of the wide steps of the Museum, those that descended from the galleries of painting, and then, after the young man had left her, smiling, looking back, waving all gayly and expressively his hat and stick, had watched him, smiling too, but with a different intensity—had kept him in sight till he passed out of the great door. She might have been waiting to see if he would turn there for a last demonstration; which was exactly what he did, renewing his cordial gesture and with his look of glad devotion,

the radiance of his young face, reaching her
across the great space, as she felt, in un-
diminished truth. Yes, so she could feel,
and she remained a minute even after he was
gone; she gazed at the empty air as if he had
filled it still, asking herself what more she
wanted and what, if it didn't signify glad devotion, his whole air could have represented.

She was at present so anxious that she
could wonder if he stepped and smiled like
that for mere relief at separation; yet if he
desired in that degree to break the spell
and escape the danger why did he keep
coming back to her, and why, for that matter, had she felt safe a moment before in letting him go? She felt safe, felt almost reck-
less—that was the proof—so long as he was
with her; but the chill came as soon as he
had gone, when she took the measure, in-
stantly, of all she yet missed. She might
now have been taking it afresh, by the testimony of her charming clouded eyes and of
the rigor that had already replaced her beautiful play of expression. Her radiance, for

the minute, had "carried" as far as his, travelling on the light wings of her brilliant prettiness—he, on his side, not being facially handsome, but only sensitive, clean and eager. Then, with its extinction, the sustaining wings dropped and hung.

She wheeled about, however, full of a purpose; she passed back through the pictured rooms, for it pleased her, this idea of a talk with Mr. Pitman—as much, that is, as anything could please a young person so troubled. It happened indeed that when she saw him rise at sight of her from the settee where he had told her five minutes before that she would find him, it was just with her nervousness that his presence seemed, as through an odd suggestion of help, to connect itself. Nothing truly would be quite so odd for her case as aid proceeding from Mr. Pitman; unless perhaps the oddity would be even greater for himself—the oddity of her having taken into her head an appeal to him.

She had had to feel alone with a vengeance —inwardly alone and miserably alarmed—

[3]

to be ready to "meet," that way, at the first
sign from him, the successor to her dim father
in her dim father's lifetime, the second of her
mother's two divorced husbands. It made
a queer relation for her; a relation that
struck her at this moment as less edifying,
less natural and graceful than it would have
been even for her remarkable mother—and
still in spite of this parent's third marriage,
her union with Mr. Connery, from whom she
was informally separated. It was at the
back of Julia's head as she approached Mr.
Pitman, or it was at least somewhere deep
within her soul, that if this last of Mrs. Connery's withdrawals from the matrimonial
yoke had received the sanction of the court
(Julia had always heard, from far back, so
much about the "Court") she herself, as
after a fashion, in that event, a party to it,
would not have had the cheek to make up—
which was how she inwardly phrased what
she was doing—to the long, lean, loose,
slightly cadaverous gentleman who was a
memory, for her, of the period fr m her

[4]

twelfth to her seventeenth year. She had
got on with him, perversely, much better
than her mother had, and the bulging misfit
of his duck waistcoat, with his trick of swing-
ing his eye-glass, at the end of an extraor-
dinarily long string, far over the scene, came
back to her as positive features of the image
of her remoter youth. Her present age—
for her later time had seen so many things
happen—gave her a perspective.

Fifty things came up as she stood there
before him, some of them floating in from
the past, others hovering with freshness:
how she used to dodge the rotary movement
made by his pince-nez while he always awk-
wardly, and kindly, and often funnily, talked
—it had once hit her rather badly in the eye;
how she used to pull down and straighten
his waistcoat, making it set a little better, a
thing of a sort her mother never did; how
friendly and familiar she must have been
with him for that, or else a forward little
minx; how she felt almost capable of doing
it again now, just to sound the right note,

[5]

and how sure she was of the way he would take it if she did; how much nicer he had clearly been, all the while, poor dear man, than his wife and the court had made it possible for him publicly to appear; how much younger, too, he now looked, in spite of his rather melancholy, his mildly-jaundiced, humorously determined sallowness and his careless assumption, everywhere, from his forehead to his exposed and relaxed blue socks, almost sky-blue, as in past days, of creases and folds and furrows that would have been perhaps tragic if they hadn't seemed rather to show, like his whimsical black eyebrows, the vague, interrogative arch.

Of course he wasn't wretched if he wasn't more sure of his wretchedness than that! Julia Bride would have been sure—had she been through what she supposed *he* had! With his thick, loose black hair, in any case, untouched by a thread of gray, and his kept gift of a certain big-boyish awkwardness— that of his taking their encounter, for instance, so amusedly, so crudely, though, as

[6]

she was not unaware, so eagerly too—he could
by no means have been so little his wife's
junior as it had been that lady's habit, after
the divorce, to represent him.   Julia had remembered him as old, since she had so constantly thought of her mother as old; which
Mrs. Connery was indeed now — for her
daughter — with her dozen years of actual
seniority to Mr. Pitman and her exquisite
hair, the densest, the finest tangle of arranged silver tendrils that had ever enhanced
the effect of a preserved complexion.

Something in the girl's vision of her quon-
dam stepfather as still comparatively young
—with the confusion, the immense element
of rectification, not to say of rank disproof,
that it introduced into Mrs. Connery's fa-
vorite picture of her own injured past—all
this worked, even at the moment, to quicken
once more the clearness and harshness of
judgment, the retrospective disgust, as she
might have called it, that had of late grown
up in her, the sense of all the folly and vanity
and vulgarity, the lies, the perversities, the

falsification of all life in the interest of who
could say what wretched frivolity, what pre-
posterous policy, amid which she had been
condemned so ignorantly, so pitifully to sit,
to walk, to grope, to flounder, from the very
dawn of her consciousness. Didn't poor Mr.
Pitman just touch the sensitive nerve of it
when, taking her in with his facetious, cau-
tious eyes, he spoke to her, right out, of the
old, old story, the everlasting little wonder
of her beauty?

"Why, you know, you've grown up so
lovely—you're the prettiest girl I've ever
seen!" Of course she was the prettiest girl
he had ever seen; she was the prettiest girl
people much more privileged than he had
ever seen; since when hadn't she been passing for the prettiest girl any one had ever
seen? She had lived in that, from far back,
from year to year, from day to day and from
hour to hour—she had lived for it and literally *by* it, as who should say; but Mr. Pitman was somehow more illuminating than
he knew, with the present lurid light that

he cast upon old dates, old pleas, old values,
and old mysteries, not to call them old
abysses: it had rolled over her in a swift
wave, with the very sight of him, that her
mother couldn't possibly have been right
about him—as about what in the world had
she ever been right?—so that in fact he was
simply offered her there as one more of Mrs.
Connery's lies. She might have thought she
knew them all by this time; but he represented for her, coming in just as he did, a
fresh discovery, and it was this contribution
of freshness that made her somehow feel she
liked him. It was she herself who, for so
long, with her retained impression, had been
right about him; and the rectification he
represented had *all* shone out of him, ten
minutes before, on his catching her eye
while she moved through the room with Mr.
French. She had never doubted of his prob-
able faults—which her mother had vividly
depicted as the basest of vices; since some
of them, and the most obvious (not the vices,
but the faults) were written on him as he

stood there: notably, for instance, the exas-
perating "business slackness" of which Mrs.
Connery had, before the tribunal, made so
pathetically much. It might have been,
for that matter, the very business slackness
that affected Julia as presenting its friendly
breast, in the form of a cool loose sociability,
to her own actual tension; though it was
also true for her, after they had exchanged
fifty words, that he had as well his inward
fever and that, if he was perhaps wondering
what was so particularly the matter with
her, she could make out not less that something was the matter with *him*.   It had been
vague, yet it had been intense, the mute reflection, "Yes, I'm going to like him, and
he's going somehow to help me!" that had
directed her steps so straight to him.   She
was sure even then of this, that he wouldn't
put to her a query about his former wife,
that he took to-day no grain of interest in
Mrs. Connery; that his interest, such as it
was—and he couldn't look *quite* like that,
to Julia Bride's expert perception, without

something in the nature of a new one—
would be a thousand times different.

It was as a value of *disproof* that his
worth meanwhile so rapidly grew: the good
sight of him, the good sound and sense of
him, such as they were, demolished at a
stroke so blessedly much of the horrid inconvenience of the past that she thought of
him, she clutched at him, for a *general* saving
use, an application as sanative, as redemptive
as some universal healing wash, precious
even to the point of perjury if perjury should
be required. That was the terrible thing,
that had been the inward pang with which
she watched Basil French recede: perjury
would have to come in somehow and somewhere—oh so quite certainly!—before the so
strange, so rare young man, truly smitten
though she believed him, could be made to
rise to the occasion, before her measureless
prize could be assured. It was present to
her, it had been present a hundred times,
that if there had only been some one to (as
it were) "deny everything" the situation

might yet be saved.   She so needed some one
to lie for her—ah, she so needed some one
to lie! Her mother's version of everything,
her mother's version of anything, had been
at the best, as they said, discounted; and she
herself could but show, of course, for an interested party, however much she might
claim to be none the less a decent girl—to
whatever point, that is, after all that had
both remotely and recently happened, pre-
sumptions of anything to be called decency
could come in.

After what had recently happened—the
two or three indirect but so worrying questions Mr. French had put to her—it would
only be some thoroughly detached friend or
witness who might effectively testify. An
odd form of detachment certainly would
reside, for Mr. Pitman's evidential character,
in her mother's having so publicly and so
brilliantly—though, thank the powers, all
off in North Dakota!—severed their connection with him; and yet mightn't it do *her*
some good, even if the harm it might do her

mother were so little ambiguous? The more
her mother had got divorced—with her
dreadful cheap-and-easy second performance
in that line and her present extremity of
alienation from Mr. Connery, which enfolded
beyond doubt the germ of a third petition on
one side or the other—the more her mother
had distinguished herself in the field of folly
the worse for her own prospect with the
Frenches, whose minds she had guessed to
be accessible, and with such an effect of dis-
simulated suddenness, to some insidious
poison.

It was very unmistakable, in other words,
that the more dismissed and detached Mr.
Pitman should have come to appear, the
more as divorced, or at least as divorcing, his
before-time wife would by the same stroke
figure—so that it was here poor Julia could
but lose herself. The crazy divorces only,
or the half-dozen successive and still crazier
engagements only — gathered fruit, bitter
fruit, of her own incredibly allowed, her own
insanely fostered frivolity—either of these

two groups of skeletons at the banquet
might singly be dealt with; but the combina-
tion, the fact of each party's having been so
mixed-up with whatever was least present-
able for the other, the fact of their having
so shockingly amused themselves together,
made all present steering resemble the classic
middle course between Scylla and Charybdis.

It was not, however, that she felt wholly
a fool in having obeyed this impulse to pick
up again her kind old friend. *She* at least
had never divorced him, and her horrid little
filial evidence in court had been but the
chatter of a parrakeet, of precocious plumage
and croak, repeating words earnestly taught
her and that she could scarce even pro-
nounce. Therefore, as far as steering went,
he *must* for the hour take a hand. She
might actually have wished in fact that he
shouldn't now have seemed so tremendously
struck with her; since it was an extraordinary situation for a girl, this crisis of her
fortune, this positive wrong that the flagran-
cy, what she would have been ready to

call the very vulgarity, of her good looks
might do her at a moment when it was vital
she should hang as straight as a picture on
the wall.   Had it ever yet befallen any young
woman in the world to wish with secret intensity that she might have been, for her
convenience, a shade less inordinately pretty?
She had come to that, to this view of the
bane, the primal curse, of their lavish physical outfit, which had included everything
and as to which she lumped herself resent-
fully with her mother.   The only thing was
that her mother was, thank goodness, still so
much prettier, still so assertively, so publicly, so trashily, so ruinously pretty.   Wonderful the small grimness with which Julia
Bride put off on this parent the middle-aged
maximum of their case and the responsi-
bility of their defect.   It cost her so little to
recognize in Mrs. Connery at forty-seven,
and in spite, or perhaps indeed just by reason, of the arranged silver tendrils which
were so like some rare bird's-nest in a morning frost, a facile supremacy for the dazzling

effect—it cost her so little that her view even
rather exaggerated the lustre of the different maternal items. She would have put
it *all* off if possible, all off on other shoulders
and on other graces and other morals than
her own, the burden of physical charm that
had made so easy a ground, such a native
favoring air, for the aberrations which, ap-
parently inevitable and without far consequences at the time, had yet at this junc-
ture so much better not have been.

She could have worked it out at her leisure,
to the last link of the chain, the way their
prettiness had set them trap after trap, all
along—had foredoomed them to awful ineptitude. When you were as pretty as that
you could, by the whole idiotic consensus,
be nothing *but* pretty; and when you were
nothing "but" pretty you could get into
nothing but tight places, out of which you
could then scramble by nothing but masses
of fibs. And there was no one, all the while,
who wasn't eager to egg you on, eager to
make you pay to the last cent the price of

your beauty. What creature would ever for
a moment help you to behave as if something
that dragged in its wake a bit less of a lum-
bering train would, on the whole, have been
better for you? The consequences of being
plain were only negative—you failed of this
and that; but the consequences of being as
they were, what were these but endless?
though indeed, as far as failing went, your
beauty too could let you in for enough of it.
Who, at all events, would ever for a moment
credit you, in the luxuriance of that beauty,
with the study, on your own side, of such
truths as these? Julia Bride could, at the
point she had reached, positively ask herself
this even while lucidly conscious of the inimitable, the triumphant and attested pro-
jection, all round her, of her exquisite image.
It was only Basil French who had at last,
in his doubtless dry, but all distinguished
way—the way surely, as it was borne in upon
her, of all the blood of all the Frenches—
stepped out of the vulgar rank. It was only
he who, by the trouble she discerned in him,

had made her see certain things. It was only for him—and not a bit ridiculously, but just beautifully, almost sublimely—that their being "nice," her mother and she between them, had *not* seemed to profit by their being so furiously handsome.

This had, ever so grossly and ever so tiresomely, satisfied every one else; since every one had thrust upon them, had imposed upon them, as by a great cruel conspiracy, their silliest possibilities; fencing them in to these, and so not only shutting them out from others, but mounting guard at the fence, walking round and round outside it, to see they didn't escape, and admiring them, talking to them, through the rails, in mere terms of chaff, terms of chucked cakes and apples—as if they had been antelopes or zebras, or even some superior sort of performing, of dancing, bear. It had been reserved for Basil French to strike her as willing to let go, so to speak, a pound or two of this fatal treasure if he might only have got in exchange for it an ounce or so more

of their so much less obvious and less pub-
lished personal history. Yes, it described
him to say that, in addition to all the rest of
him, and of *his* personal history, and of his
family, and of theirs, in addition to their
social posture, as that of a serried phalanx,
and to their notoriously enormous wealth
and crushing respectability, she might have
been ever so much less lovely for him if she
had been only—well, a little prepared to
answer questions. And it wasn't as if quiet,
cultivated, earnest, public-spirited, brought
up in Germany, infinitely travelled, awfully
like a high-caste Englishman, and all the
other pleasant things, it wasn't as if he didn't
love to be with her, to look at her, just as
she was; for he loved it exactly as much, so
far as that footing simply went, as any free
and foolish youth who had ever made the
last demonstration of it. It was that marriage was, for him—and for them all, the
serried Frenches—a great matter, a goal to
which a man of intelligence, a real shy,
beautiful man of the world, didn't hop on

one foot, didn't skip and jump, as if he were playing an urchins' game, but toward which he proceeded with a deep and anxious, a noble and highly just deliberation.

For it was one thing to stare at a girl till she was bored with it, it was one thing to take her to the Horse Show and the Opera, and to send her flowers by the stack, and chocolates by the ton, and "great" novels, the very latest and greatest, by the dozen; but something quite other to hold open for her, with eyes attached to eyes, the gate, moving on such stiff silver hinges, of the grand square forecourt of the palace of wedlock. The state of being "engaged" represented to him the introduction to this precinct of some young woman with whom his outside parley would have had the duration, distinctly, of his own convenience. That might be cold-blooded if one chose to think so; but nothing of another sort would equal the high ceremony and dignity and decency, above all the grand gallantry and finality, of their then passing in. Poor Julia

could have blushed red, before that view,
with the memory of the way the forecourt,
as she now imagined it, had been dishonored
by her younger romps. She had tumbled
over the wall with this, that, and the other
raw playmate, and had played "tag" and
leap-frog, as she might say, from corner to
corner. That would be the "history" with
which, in case of definite demand, she should
be able to supply Mr. French: that she had
already, again and again, any occasion of-
fering, chattered and scuffled over ground
provided, according to his idea, for walking
the gravest of minuets. If that then had
been all their *kind* of history, hers and her
mother's, at least there was plenty of it: it
was the superstructure raised on the other
group of facts, those of the order of their having been always so perfectly pink and white,
so perfectly possessed of clothes, so perfectly
splendid, so perfectly idiotic. These things
had been the "points" of antelope and zebra;
putting Mrs. Connery for the zebra, as the
more remarkably striped or spotted. Such

were the *data* Basil French's inquiry would elicit: her own six engagements and her mother's three nullified marriages—nine nice distinct little horrors in all. What on earth was to be done about them?

It was notable, she was afterward to recognize, that there had been nothing of the famous business slackness in the positive pounce with which Mr. Pitman put it to her that, as soon as he had made her out "for sure," identified her there as old Julia grown-up and gallivanting with a new admirer, a smarter young fellow than ever yet, he had had the inspiration of her being exactly the good girl to help him. She certainly found him strike the hour again, with these vulgarities of tone — forms of speech that her mother had anciently described as by themselves, once he had opened the whole battery, sufficient ground for putting him away. Full, however, of the use she should have for him, she wasn't going to mind trifles. What she really gasped at was that, so oddly, he was

ahead of her at the start. "Yes, I want
something of you, Julia, and I want it right
now: you can do me a turn, and I'm blest
if my luck—which has once or twice been
pretty good, you know—hasn't sent you to
me." She knew the luck he meant—that
of her mother's having so enabled him to get
rid of her; but it was the nearest allusion of
the merely invidious kind that he would
make. It had thus come to our young woman on the spot and by divination: the service
he desired of her matched with remarkable
closeness what she had so promptly taken
into her head to name to himself—to name
in her own interest, though deterred as yet
from having brought it right out. She had
been prevented by his speaking, the first
thing, in that way, as if he had known Mr.
French—which surprised her till he ex-
plained that every one in New York knew by
appearance a young man of his so-quoted
wealth ("What did she take them all in
New York then *for?*") and of whose marked
attention to her he had moreover, for him-

self, round at clubs and places, lately heard.
This had accompanied the inevitable free
question "Was she engaged to *him* now?"—
which she had in fact almost welcomed as
holding out to her the perch of opportunity.
She was waiting to deal with it properly, but
meanwhile he had gone on, and to such effect
that it took them but three minutes to turn
out, on either side, like a pair of pickpockets
comparing, under shelter, their day's booty,
the treasures of design concealed about their
persons.

"I want you to tell the truth for me—as
you only can.   I want you to say that I was
really all right—as right as you know; and
that I simply acted like an angel in a story-
book, gave myself away to have it over."

"Why, my dear man," Julia cried, "you
take the wind straight out of my sails!
What I'm here to ask of *you* is that you'll
confess to having been even a worse fiend
than you were shown up for; to having made
it impossible mother should *not* take pro-
ceedings."   There!—she had brought it out,

and with the sense of their situation turning
to high excitement for her in the teeth of his
droll stare, his strange grin, his characteristic
"Lordy, lordy! What good will that do
you?" She was prepared with her clear
statement of reasons for her appeal, and
feared so he might have better ones for his
own that all her story came in a flash.
"Well, Mr. Pitman, I want to get married
this time, by way of a change; but you see
we've been such fools that, when something
really good at last comes up, it's too dreadfully awkward. The fools we were capable
of being—well, you know better than any
one: unless perhaps not quite so well as Mr.
Connery. It has got to be denied," said
Julia ardently—"it has got to be denied flat.
But I can't get hold of Mr. Connery—Mr.
Connery has gone to China. Besides, if he
were here," she had ruefully to confess, "he'd
be no good—on the contrary. He wouldn't
deny anything—he'd only tell more. So
thank heaven he's away — there's *that*
amount of good! I'm not engaged yet,"

3   [25]

she went on—but he had already taken her
up.

"You're not engaged to Mr. French?" It
was all, clearly, a wondrous show for him,
but his immediate surprise, oddly, might
have been greatest for that.

"No, not to any one—for the seventh
time!" She spoke as with her head held well
up both over the shame and the pride. "Yes,
the next time I'm engaged I want something
to happen. But he's afraid; he's afraid of
what may be told him. He's dying to find
out, and yet he'd die if he did! He wants to
be talked to, but he has got to be talked to
right. You could talk to him right, Mr.
Pitman—if you only *would!* He can't get
over mother—that I feel: he loathes and
scorns divorces, and we've had first and last
too many. So if he could hear from you
that you just made her life a hell—why,"
Julia concluded, "it would be too lovely. If
she *had* to go in for another—after having
already, when I was little, divorced father—
it would 'sort of' make, don't you see? one

less.   You'd do the high-toned thing by her:
you'd say what a wretch you then were, and
that she had had to save her life.   In that
way he mayn't mind it.   Don't you see, you
sweet man?'' poor Julia pleaded. "Oh,"
she wound up as if his fancy lagged or his
scruple looked out, " of course I want you to
lie for me!''

It did indeed sufficiently stagger him. " It's
a lovely idea for the moment when I was
just saying to myself—as soon as I saw you
—that you'd speak the truth for *me!*"

"Ah, what's the matter with 'you'?"
Julia sighed with an impatience not sensibly
less sharp for her having so quickly scented
some lion in her path.

"Why, do you think there's no one in the
world but you who has seen the cup of
promised affection, of something really to be
depended on, only, at the last moment, by
the horrid jostle of your elbow, spilled all
over you?   I want to provide for my future
too as it happens; and my good friend who's
to help me to that—the most charming of

[27]

women this time—disapproves of divorce
quite as much as Mr. French. Don't you
see," Mr. Pitman candidly asked, "what that
by itself must have done toward attaching
me to her? *She* has got to be talked to—
to be told how little I could help it."

"Oh, lordy, lordy!" the girl emulously
groaned. It was such a relieving cry. "Well,
I won't talk to her!" she declared.

"You *won't*, Julia?" he pitifully echoed.
"And yet you ask of *me*—!"

His pang, she felt, was sincere; and even
more than she had guessed, for the previous
quarter of an hour he had been building up
his hope, building it with her aid for a foun-
dation. Yet was he going to see how their
testimony, on each side, would, if offered,
have to conflict? If he was to prove himself
for her sake—or, more queerly still, for that
of Basil French's high conservatism—a person whom there had been no other way of
dealing with, how could she prove him, in
this other and so different interest, a mere
gentle sacrifice to his wife's perversity? She

[28]

had, before him there, on the instant, all
acutely, a sense of rising sickness—a wan
glimmer of foresight as to the end of the
fond dream. Everything else was against
her, everything in her dreadful past—just
as if she had been a person represented by
some "emotional actress," some desperate
erring lady "hunted down" in a play; but
was that going to be the case too with her
own very decency, the fierce little residuum
deep within her, for which she was counting,
when she came to think, on so little glory or
even credit? Was this also going to turn
against her and trip her up—just to show
she was really, under the touch and the test,
as decent as any one; and with no one but
herself the wiser for it meanwhile, and no
proof to show but that, as a consequence, she
should be unmarried to the end? She put
it to Mr. Pitman quite with resentment:
"Do you mean to say you're going to be
married—?"

"Oh, my dear, I too must get engaged
first!"—he spoke with his inimitable grin.

"But that, you see, is where you come in. I've told her about you. She wants awfully to meet you. The way it happens is too lovely—that I find you just in this place. She's coming," said Mr. Pitman—and as in all the good faith of his eagerness now; "she's coming in about three minutes."

"Coming here?"

"Yes, Julia—right here. It's where we usually meet"; and he was wreathed again, this time as if for life, in his large slow smile. "She loves this place—she's awfully keen on art. Like *you*, Julia, if you haven't changed —I remember how you did love art." He looked at her quite tenderly, as to keep her up to it. "You must still of course—from the way you're here. Just let her *feel* that," the poor man fantastically urged. And then with his kind eyes on her and his good ugly mouth stretched as for delicate emphasis from ear to ear: "Every little helps!"

He made her wonder for him, ask herself, and with a certain intensity, questions she

yet hated the trouble of; as whether he were
still as moneyless as in the other time—which
was certain indeed, for any fortune he ever
would have made.   His slackness, on that
ground, stuck out of him almost as much as
if he had been of rusty or " seedy " aspect—
which, luckily for him, he wasn't at all: he
looked, in his way, like some pleasant eccen-
tric, ridiculous, but real gentleman, whose
taste might be of the queerest, but his credit
with his tailor none the less of the best.   She
wouldn't have been the least ashamed, had
their connection lasted, of going about with
him: so that what a fool, again, her mother
had been—since Mr. Connery, sorry as one
might be for him, was irrepressibly vulgar.
Julia's quickness was, for the minute, charged
with all this; but she had none the less her
feeling of the right thing to say and the right
way to say it.   If he was after a future financially assured, even as she herself so fran-
tically was, she wouldn't cast the stone.
But if he had talked about her to strange
women she couldn't be less than a little

[31]

majestic. "Who then is the person in question for you—?"

"Why, such a dear thing, Julia—Mrs.
David E. Drack. Have you heard of her?"
he almost fluted.

New York was vast, and she had not had
that advantage. "She's a widow—?"

"Oh yes: she's not—!" He caught himself up in time. "She's a real one." It was
as near as he came. But it was as if he had
been looking at her now so pathetically hard.
"Julia, she has millions."

Hard, at any rate—whether pathetic or
not — was the look she gave him back.
"Well, so has—or so *will* have—Basil French.
And more of them than Mrs. Drack, I guess,"
Julia quavered.

"Oh, I know what *they've* got!" He took
it from her—with the effect of a vague stir,
in his long person, of unwelcome embarrass-
ment. But was she going to give up because he was embarrassed? He should know
at least what he was costing her. It came
home to her own spirit more than ever; but

[32]

meanwhile he had found his footing. "I don't see how your mother matters. It isn't a question of his marrying *her*."

"No; but, constantly together as we've always been, it's a question of there being so disgustingly much to get over. If we had, for people like them, but the one ugly spot and the one weak side; if we had made, between us, but the one vulgar *kind* of mistake: well, I don't say!" She reflected with a wistfulness of note that was in itself a touching eloquence. "To have our reward in this world we've had too sweet a time. We've had it all right down here!" said Julia Bride. "I should have taken the precaution to have about a dozen fewer lovers."

"Ah, my dear, 'lovers'—!" He ever so comically attenuated.

"Well they *were!*" She quite flared up. "When you've had a ring from each (three diamonds, two pearls, and a rather bad sapphire: I've kept them all, and they tell my story!) what are you to call them?"

"Oh, rings—!" Mr. Pitman didn't call

rings anything. "I've given Mrs. Drack a ring."

Julia stared. "Then aren't you her lover?"

"That, dear child," he humorously wailed, "is what I want you to find out! But I'll handle your rings all right," he more lucidly added.

"You'll 'handle' them?"

"I'll fix your lovers. I'll lie about *them*, if that's all you want."

"Oh, about 'them'—!" She turned away with a sombre drop, seeing so little in it. "That wouldn't count — from *you!*" She saw the great shining room, with its mockery of art and "style" and security, all the things she was vainly after, and its few scattered visitors who had left them, Mr. Pitman and herself, in their ample corner, so conveniently at ease. There was only a lady in one of the far doorways, of whom she took vague note and who seemed to be looking at them. "They'd have to lie for themselves!"

"Do you mean he's capable of putting it to them?"

Mr. Pitman's tone threw discredit on that possibility, but she knew perfectly well what she meant. "Not of getting at them directly, not, as mother says, of nosing round himself; but of listening—and small blame to him!—to the horrible things other people say of me."

"But what other people?"

"Why, Mrs. George Maule, to begin with —who intensely loathes us, and who talks to his sisters, so that they may talk to *him:* which they do, all the while, I'm morally sure (hating me as they also must). But it's she who's the real reason—I mean of his holding off. She poisons the air he breathes."

"Oh well," said Mr. Pitman with easy optimism, "if Mrs. George Maule's a cat—!"

"If she's a cat she has kittens—four little spotlessly white ones, among whom she'd give her head that Mr. French should make his pick. He could do it with his eyes shut —you can't tell them apart. But she has

every name, every date, as you may say,
for my dark 'record'—as of course they all
call it: she'll be able to give him, if he brings
himself to ask her, every fact in its order.
And all the while, don't you see? there's no
one to speak *for* me."

It would have touched a harder heart than
her loose friend's to note the final flush of
clairvoyance witnessing this assertion and
under which her eyes shone as with the rush
of quick tears. He stared at her, and at
what this did for the deep charm of her
prettiness, as in almost witless admiration.
"But can't you—lovely as you are, you
beautiful thing!—speak for yourself?"

"Do you mean can't I tell the lies? No,
then, I can't—and I wouldn't if I could.
I don't lie myself, you know—as it happens;
and it could represent to him then about the
only thing, the only bad one, I don't do.
I *did*—'lovely as I am'!—have my regular
time; I wasn't so hideous that I couldn't!
Besides, do you imagine he'd come and ask
me?"

[36]

"Gad, I wish he would, Julia!" said Mr. Pitman with his kind eyes on her.

"Well then, I'd tell him!" And she held her head again high. "But he won't."

It fairly distressed her companion. "Doesn't he want then to know——?"

"He wants *not* to know. He wants to be told without asking—told, I mean, that each of the stories, those that have come to him, is a fraud and a libel. *Qui s'excuse s'accuse*, don't they say?—so that do you see me breaking out to him, unprovoked, with four or five what-do-you-call-'ems, the things mother used to have to prove in court, a set of neat little 'alibis' in a row? How can I get hold of so *many* precious gentlemen, to turn them on? How can *they* want everything fished up?"

She had paused for her climax, in the intensity of these considerations; which gave Mr. Pitman a chance to express his honest faith. "Why, my sweet child, they'd be just glad——!"

It determined in her loveliness almost a

sudden glare. "Glad to swear they never had anything to do with such a creature? Then *I'd* be glad to swear they had lots!"

His persuasive smile, though confessing to bewilderment, insisted. "Why, my love, they've got to swear either one thing or the other."

"They've got to keep out of the way—that's *their* view of it, I guess," said Julia. "Where *are* they, please—now that they *may* be wanted? If you'd like to hunt them up for me you're very welcome." With which, for the moment, over the difficult case, they faced each other helplessly enough. And she added to it now the sharpest ache of her despair. "He knows about Murray Brush. The others"—and her pretty white-gloved hands and charming pink shoulders gave them up—"may go hang!"

"Murray Brush—?" It had opened Mr. Pitman's eyes.

"Yes—yes; I do mind *him*."

"Then what's the matter with his at least rallying—?"

[38]

"The matter is that, being ashamed of himself, as he well might, he left the country as soon as he could and has stayed away. The matter is that he's in Paris or somewhere, and that if you expect him to come home for me—!" She had already dropped, however, as at Mr. Pitman's look.

"Why, you foolish thing, Murray Brush is in New York!" It had quite brightened him up.

"He has come back—?"

"Why, sure! I saw him—when was it? Tuesday!—on the Jersey boat." Mr. Pitman rejoiced in his news. "*He's* your man!"

Julia too had been affected by it; it had brought, in a rich wave, her hot color back. But she gave the strangest dim smile. "He *was!*"

"Then get hold of him, and—if he's a gentleman—he'll prove for you, to the hilt, that he wasn't."

It lighted in her face, the kindled train of this particular sudden suggestion, a glow, a sharpness of interest, that had deepened

the next moment, while she gave a slow and
sad head-shake, to a greater strangeness yet.
"He isn't a gentleman."

"Ah, lordy, lordy!" Mr. Pitman again
sighed. He struggled out of it but only into
the vague. "Oh then, if he's a pig—!"

"You see there are only a few gentlemen
—not enough to go round—and that makes
them count so!" It had thrust the girl herself, for that matter, into depths; but whether
most of memory or of roused purpose he had
no time to judge—aware as he suddenly was
of a shadow (since he mightn't perhaps too
quickly call it a light) across the heaving
surface of their question. It fell upon Julia's
face, fell with the sound of the voice he so
well knew, but which could only be odd to
her for all it immediately assumed.

"There are indeed very few—and one
mustn't try *them* too much!" Mrs. Drack,
who had supervened while they talked, stood,
in monstrous magnitude—at least to Julia's
reimpressed eyes—between them: she was
the lady our young woman had descried

across the room, and she had drawn near
while the interest of their issue so held them.
We have seen the act of observation and
that of reflection alike swift in Julia—once
her subject was within range—and she had
now, with all her perceptions at the acutest,
taken in, by a single stare, the strange
presence to a happy connection with which
Mr. Pitman aspired and which had thus sail-
ed, with placid majesty, into their troubled
waters.   She was clearly not shy, Mrs.
David E. Drack, yet neither was she omi-
nously bold; she was bland and "good," Julia
made sure at a glance, and of a large complacency, as the good and the bland are apt
to be—a large complacency, a large sen-
timentality, a large innocent, elephantine
archness: she fairly rioted in that dimension
of size.   Habited in an extraordinary quantity of stiff and lustrous black brocade, with
enhancements, of every description, that
twinkled and tinkled, that rustled and rum-
bled with her least movement, she presented
a huge, hideous, pleasant face, a featureless

desert in a remote quarter of which the
disproportionately small eyes might have
figured a pair of rash adventurers all but
buried in the sand. They reduced themselves when she smiled to barely discernible
points—a couple of mere tiny emergent heads
—though the foreground of the scene, as if
to make up for it, gaped with a vast benevolence. In a word Julia saw — and as if
she had needed nothing more; saw Mr. Pitman's opportunity, saw her own, saw the
exact nature both of Mrs. Drack's circum-
spection and of Mrs. Drack's sensibility, saw
even, glittering there in letters of gold and
as a part of the whole metallic coruscation,
the large figure of her income, largest of all
her attributes, and (though perhaps a little
more as a luminous blur beside all this) the
mingled ecstasy and agony of Mr. Pitman's
hope and Mr. Pitman's fear.

He was introducing them, with his pathetic belief in the virtue for every occasion, in
the solvent for every trouble, of an extrava-
gant, genial, professional humor; he was

naming her to Mrs. Drack as the charming
young friend he had told her so much about
and who had been as an angel to him in a
weary time; he was saying that the loveliest
chance in the world, this accident of a meeting in those promiscuous halls, had placed
within his reach the pleasure of bringing
them together. It didn't indeed matter,
Julia felt, what he was saying: he conveyed
everything, as far as she was concerned, by
a moral pressure as unmistakable as if, for
a symbol of it, he had thrown himself on her
neck. Above all, meanwhile, this high consciousness prevailed—that the good lady
herself, however huge she loomed, had en-
tered, by the end of a minute, into a condi-
tion as of suspended weight and arrested
mass, stilled to artless awe by the fact of her
vision. Julia had practised almost to lassi-
tude the art of tracing in the people who
looked at her the impression promptly se-
quent; but it was a striking point that if, in
irritation, in depression, she felt that the
lighted eyes of men, stupid at their clearest,

had given her pretty well all she should ever
care for, she could still gather a freshness
from the tribute of her own sex, still care to
see her reflection in the faces of women.
Never, probably, never would that sweet be
tasteless—with such a straight grim spoon
was it mostly administered, and so flavored
and strengthened by the competence of their
eyes. Women knew so much best *how* a
woman surpassed—how and where and why,
with no touch or torment of it lost on them;
so that as it produced mainly and primarily
the instinct of aversion, the sense of extract-
ing the recognition, of gouging out the hom-
age, was on the whole the highest crown one's
felicity could wear. Once in a way, however, the grimness beautifully dropped, the
jealousy failed: the admiration was all there
and the poor plain sister handsomely paid it.
It had never been so paid, she was presently
certain, as by this great generous object of
Mr. Pitman's flame, who without optical aid,
it well might have seemed, nevertheless entirely grasped her—might in fact, all benev-

olently, have been groping her over as by
some huge mild proboscis. She gave Mrs.
Drack pleasure in short; and who could say
of what other pleasures the poor lady hadn't
been cheated?

It was somehow a muddled world in which
one of her conceivable joys, at this time of
day, would be to marry Mr. Pitman—to say
nothing of a state of things in which this
gentleman's own fancy could invest such a
union with rapture. That, however, was
their own mystery, and Julia, with each instant, was more and more clear about hers:
so remarkably primed in fact, at the end of
three minutes, that though her friend, and
though *his* friend, were both saying things,
many things and perhaps quite wonderful
things, she had no free attention for them
and was only rising and soaring. She was
rising to her value, she was soaring *with* it
—the value Mr. Pitman almost convulsively
imputed to her, the value that consisted for
her of being so unmistakably the most dazzling image Mrs. Drack had ever beheld.

These were the uses, for Julia, in fine, of
adversity; the range of Mrs. Drack's ex-
perience might have been as small as the
measure of her presence was large: Julia was
at any rate herself in face of the occasion of
her life, and, after all her late repudiations
and reactions, had perhaps never yet known
the quality of this moment's success. She
hadn't an idea of what, on either side, had
been uttered—beyond Mr. Pitman's allusion
to her having befriended him of old: she simply held his companion with her radiance
and knew she might be, for her effect, as
irrelevant as she chose. It was relevant to
do what he wanted—it was relevant to dish
herself. She did it now with a kind of passion, to say nothing of her knowing, with it,
that every word of it added to her beauty.
She gave him away in short, up to the hilt, for
any use of her own, and should have nothing to clutch at now but the possibility of
Murray Brush.

"He says I was good to him, Mrs. Drack;
and I'm sure I hope I was, since I should be

"HE SAYS I WAS GOOD TO HIM, MRS. DRACK"

ashamed to be anything else.   If I could be
good to him now I should be glad—that's
just what, a while ago, I rushed up to him
here, after so long, to give myself the pleasure
of saying.   I saw him years ago very particularly, very miserably tried—and I saw
the way he took it.   I did see it, you dear
man," she sublimely went on—" I saw it for
all you may protest, for all you may hate me
to talk about you!   I saw you behave like a
gentleman—since Mrs. Drack agrees with me,
so charmingly, that there are not many to
be met.   I don't know whether you care,
Mrs. Drack"—she abounded, she revelled
in the name—" but I've always remembered
it of him: that under the most extraordinary
provocation he was decent and patient and
brave.   No appearance of anything different
matters, for I speak of what I *know*.   Of
course I'm nothing and nobody; I'm only a
poor frivolous girl, but I was very close to
him at the time.   That's all my little story
—if it *should* interest you at all."   She
measured every beat of her wing, she knew

how high she was going and paused only
when it was quite vertiginous. Here she
hung a moment as in the glare of the upper
blue; which was but the glare—what else
could it be?—of the vast and magnificent
attention of both her auditors, hushed, on
their side, in the splendor she emitted. She
had at last to steady herself and she scarce
knew afterwards at what rate or in what way
she had still inimitably come down—her
own eyes fixed all the while on the very
figure of her achievement. She had sacrificed her mother on the altar—proclaimed
her as false and cruel; and if that didn't
"fix" Mr. Pitman, as he would have said
—well, it was all she could do. But the
cost of her action already somehow came
back to her with increase; the dear gaunt
man fairly wavered, to her sight, in the glory
of it, as if signalling at her, with wild glee-
ful arms, from some mount of safety, while
the massive lady just spread and spread like
a rich fluid a bit helplessly spilt. It was
really the outflow of the poor woman's

[48]

honest response, into which she seemed to melt, and Julia scarce distinguished the two apart even for her taking gracious leave of each. "Good-bye, Mrs. Drack; I'm awfully happy to have met you"—like as not it was for this she had grasped Mr. Pitman's hand. And then to him or to her, it didn't matter which, "Good-bye, dear good Mr. Pitman—hasn't it been nice after so long?"

II

ULIA floated even to her own sense swanlike away—she left in her wake their fairly stupefied submission: it was as if she had, by an exquisite authority, now *placed* them, each for each, and they would have nothing to do but be happy together. Never had she so exulted as on this ridiculous occasion in the noted items of her beauty. *Le compte y était*, as they used to say in Paris—every one of them, for her immediate employment, was there; and there was something in it after all. It didn't necessarily, this sum of thumping little figures, imply charm—especially for "refined" people: nobody knew better than Julia that inexpressible charm and quotable "charms" (quotable like prices, rates, shares,

or whatever, the things they dealt in down-
town) are two distinct categories; the safest
thing for the latter being, on the whole, that
it might include the former, and the great
strength of the former being that it might
perfectly dispense with the latter. Mrs.
Drack was not refined, not the least little
bit; but what would be the case with Murray
Brush now—after his three years of Europe?
He had done so what he liked with her—
which had seemed so then just the meaning, hadn't it? of their being "engaged"
—that he had made her not see, while the
absurdity lasted (the absurdity of their pre-
tending to believe they could marry without
a cent) how little he was of metal without
alloy: this had come up for her, remarkably,
but afterwards—come up for her as she
looked back. Then she had drawn her
conclusion, which was one of the many that
Basil French had made her draw. It was a
queer service Basil was going to have rendered her, this having made everything she
had ever done impossible, if he wasn't going

to give her a new chance. If he was it was doubtless right enough. On the other hand Murray might have improved, if such a quantity of alloy, as she called it, *were*, in any man, reducible, and if Paris were the place all happily to reduce it. She had her doubts—anxious and aching on the spot, and had expressed them to Mr. Pitman: certainly, of old, he had been more open to the quotable than to the inexpressible, to charms than to charm. If she could try the quotable, however, and with such a grand result, on Mrs. Drack, she couldn't now on Murray—in respect to whom everything had changed. So that if he hadn't a sense for the subtler appeal, the appeal appreciable by people *not* vulgar, on which alone she could depend, what on earth would become of her? She could but yearningly hope, at any rate, as she made up her mind to write to him immediately at his club. It was a question of the right sensibility in him. Perhaps he would have acquired it in Europe.

Two days later indeed—for he had promptly and charmingly replied, keeping with alac-
rity the appointment she had judged best
to propose for a morning hour in a seques-
tered alley of the Park—two days later she
was to be struck well-nigh to alarm by everything he had acquired: so much it seemed
to make that it threatened somehow a com-
plication, and her plan, so far as she had
arrived at one, dwelt in the desire above all
to simplify. She wanted no grain more of
extravagance or excess of anything—risk-
ing as she had done, none the less, a recall of
ancient license in proposing to Murray such
a place of meeting. She had her reasons—
she wished intensely to discriminate: Basil
French had several times waited on her at
her mother's habitation, their horrible flat
which was so much too far up and too near
the East Side; he had dined there and lunched
there and gone with her thence to other
places, notably to see pictures, and had in
particular adjourned with her twice to the
Metropolitan Museum, in which he took a

[53]

great interest, in which she professed a de-
light, and their second visit to which had
wound up in her encounter with Mr. Pitman, after her companion had yielded, at
her urgent instance, to an exceptional need
of keeping a business engagement. She
mightn't, in delicacy, in decency, entertain
Murray Brush where she had entertained
Mr. French—she was given over now to
these exquisite perceptions and proprieties
and bent on devoutly observing them; and
Mr. French, by good-luck, had never been
with her in the Park: partly because he had
never pressed it, and partly because she
would have held off if he had, so haunted
were those devious paths and favoring
shades by the general echo of her untram-
melled past. If he had never suggested
their taking a turn there this was because,
quite divinably, he held it would commit
him further than he had yet gone; and if
she on her side had practised a like reserve
it was because the place reeked for her, as
she inwardly said, with old associations.

It reeked with nothing so much perhaps as
with the memories evoked by the young
man who now awaited her in the nook she
had been so competent to indicate; but in
what corner of the town, should she look for
them, wouldn't those footsteps creak back
into muffled life, and to what expedient
would she be reduced should she attempt
to avoid all such tracks? The Museum was
full of tracks, tracks by the hundred—the
way really she had knocked about!—but
she had to see people somewhere, and she
couldn't pretend to dodge every ghost.

All she could do was not to make confusion, make mixtures, of the living; though
she asked herself enough what mixture she
mightn't find herself to have prepared if Mr.
French should, not so very impossibly, for
a restless, roaming man—*her* effect on him!
—happen to pass while she sat there with the
mustachioed personage round whose name
Mrs. Maule would probably have caused det-
rimental anecdote most thickly to cluster.
There existed, she was sure, a mass of

luxuriant legend about the "lengths" her
engagement with Murray Brush had gone;
she could herself fairly feel them in the air,
these streamers of evil, black flags flown as
in warning, the vast redundancy of so cheap
and so dingy social bunting, in fine, that
flapped over the stations she had successive-
ly moved away from and which were empty
now, for such an ado, even to grotesqueness.
The vivacity of that conviction was what
had at present determined her, while it was
the way he listened after she had quickly
broken ground, while it was the special
character of the interested look in his handsome face, handsomer than ever yet, that
represented for her the civilization he had
somehow taken on.   Just so it was the quantity of that gain, in its turn, that had at the
end of ten minutes begun to affect her as
holding up a light to the wide reach of her
step.   "There was never anything the least
serious between us, not a sign or a scrap,
do you mind? of anything beyond the merest
pleasant friendly acquaintance; and if you're

"THERE NEVER WAS ANYTHING THE LEAST SERIOUS BETWEEN US"

not ready to go to the stake on it for me you
may as well know in time what it is you'll
probably cost me."

She had immediately plunged, measuring
her effect and having thought it well over;
and what corresponded to her question of
his having become a better person to appeal
to was the appearance of interest she had so
easily created in him. She felt on the spot
the difference that made—it was indeed his
form of being more civilized: it was the sense
in which Europe in general and Paris in particular had made him develop. By every
calculation—and her calculations, based on
the intimacy of her knowledge, had been
many and deep—he would help her the better
the more intelligent he should have become;
yet she was to recognize later on that the
first chill of foreseen disaster had been
caught by her as, at a given moment, this
greater refinement of his attention seemed
to exhale it. It was just what she had wanted—"if I can only get him interested—!" so
that, this proving quite vividly possible,

why did the light it lifted strike her as lurid? Was it partly by reason of his inordinate romantic good looks, those of a gallant, genial conqueror, but which, involving so glossy a brownness of eye, so manly a crispness of curl, so red-lipped a radiance of smile, so natural a bravery of port, prescribed to any response he might facially, might expressively, make a sort of florid, disproportionate amplitude? The explanation, in any case, didn't matter; he was going to mean well— that she could feel, and also that he had meant better in the past, presumably, than he had managed to convince her of his doing at the time: the oddity she hadn't now reckoned with was this fact that from the moment he did advertise an interest it should show almost as what she would have called weird. It made a change in him that didn't go with the rest—as if he had broken his nose or put on spectacles, lost his handsome hair or sacrificed his splendid mustache: her conception, her necessity, as she saw, had been that something should be added to

him for her use, but nothing for his own
alteration.

He had affirmed himself, and his character, and his temper, and his health, and
his appetite, and his ignorance, and his ob-
stinacy, and his whole charming, coarse,
heartless personality, during their engagement, by twenty forms of natural emphasis,
but never by emphasis of interest. How
in fact could you feel interest unless you
should know, within you, some dim stir of
imagination? There was nothing in the
world of which Murray Brush was less capable than of such a dim stir, because you
only began to imagine when you felt some
approach to a need to understand. *He* had
never felt it; for hadn't he been born, to his
personal vision, with that perfect intuition
of everything which reduces all the suggested
preliminaries of judgment to the imperti-
nence—when it's a question of your entering
your house—of a dumpage of bricks at your
door? He had had, in short, neither to
imagine nor to perceive, because he had,

from the first pulse of his intelligence, simply and supremely known: so that, at this hour, face to face with him, it came over her that she had, in their old relation, dispensed with any such convenience of comprehension on his part even to a degree she had not measured at the time. What therefore must he not have seemed to her as a form of life, a form of avidity and activity, blatantly successful in its own conceit, that he could have dazzled her so against the interest of her very faculties and functions? Strangely and richly historic all that backward mystery, and only leaving for her mind the wonder of such a mixture of possession and detachment as they would clearly to-day both know. For each to be so little at last to the other when, during months together, the idea of all abundance, all quantity, had been, for each, drawn from the other and addressed to the other—what was it monstrously like but some fantastic act of getting rid of a person by going to lock yourself up in the *sanctum sanctorum*

of that person's house, amid every evidence
of that person's habits and nature? What
was going to happen, at any rate, was that
Murray would show himself as beautifully
and consciously understanding—and it would
be prodigious that Europe should have in-
oculated him with that delicacy. Yes, he
wouldn't claim to know now till she had told
him—an aid to performance he had surely
never before waited for, or been indebted to,
from any one; and then, so knowing, he
would charmingly endeavor to "meet," to
oblige and to gratify. He would find it,
her case, ever so worthy of his benevolence,
and would be literally inspired to reflect
that he must hear about it first.

She let him hear then everything, in spite
of feeling herself slip, while she did so, to
some doom as yet incalculable; she went on
very much as she had done for Mr. Pitman
and Mrs. Drack, with the rage of despera-
tion and, as she was afterwards to call it
to herself, the fascination of the abyss. She
didn't know, couldn't have said at the time,

why his projected benevolence should have
had most so the virtue to scare her: he would
patronize her, as an effect of her vividness,
if not of her charm, and would do this with
all high intention, finding her case, or rather
their case, their funny old case, taking on of
a sudden such refreshing and edifying life,
to the last degree curious and even impor-
tant; but there were gaps of connection between this and the intensity of the perception here overtaking her that she shouldn't
be able to move in *any* direction without
dishing herself. That she couldn't afford it
where she had got to—couldn't afford the
deplorable vulgarity of having been so many
times informally affianced and contracted
(putting it only at that, at its being by the
new lights and fashions so unpardonably
vulgar): he took this from her without turning, as she might have said, a hair; except
just to indicate, with his new superiority,
that he felt the distinguished appeal and
notably the pathos of it. He still took it
from her that she hoped nothing, as it were,

from any other *alibi*—the people to drag
into court being too many and too scattered;
but that, as it was with him, Murray Brush,
she had been *most* vulgar, most everything
she had better not have been, so she depended on him for the innocence it was actually vital she should establish. He flushed
or frowned or winced no more at that than
he did when she once more fairly emptied
her satchel and, quite as if they had been
Nancy and the Artful Dodger, or some
nefarious pair of that sort, talking things
over in the manner of *Oliver Twist*, re-
vealed to him the fondness of her view
that, could she but have produced a cleaner
slate, she might by this time have pulled
it off with Mr. French. Yes, he let her
in that way sacrifice her honorable connection with him—all the more honorable
for being so completely at an end—to the
crudity of her plan for not missing another connection, so much more brilliant
than what he offered, and for bringing
another man, with whom she so invidiously
[63]

and unflatteringly compared him, into her
greedy life.

There was only a moment during which,
by a particular lustrous look she had never
had from him before, he just made her wonder which turn he was going to take; she
felt, however, as safe as was consistent with
her sense of having probably but added to
her danger, when he brought out, the next
instant: "Don't you seem to take the ground
that we were guilty—that *you* were ever
guilty—of something we shouldn't have
been? What did we ever do that was secret,
or underhand, or any way not to be acknowl-
edged? What did we do but exchange our
young vows with the best faith in the world
—publicly, rejoicingly, with the full assent
of every one connected with us? I mean of
course," he said with his grave kind smile,
"till we broke off so completely because we
found that—practically, financially, on the
hard worldly basis—we couldn't work it.
What harm, in the sight of God or man, Julia,"
he asked in his fine rich way, "did we ever do?"

She gave him back his look, turning pale. "Am I talking of *that?* Am I talking of what *we* know? I'm talking of what others feel—of what they *have* to feel; of what it's just enough for them to know not to be able to get over it, once they do really know it. How do they know what *didn't* pass between us, with all the opportunities we had? That's none of their business—if we were idiots enough, on the top of everything! What you may or mayn't have done doesn't count, for *you;* but there are people for whom it's loathsome that a girl should have gone on like that from one person to another and still pretend to be—well, all that a nice girl is supposed to be. It's as if we had but just waked up, mother and I, to such a re-markable prejudice; and now we have it— when we could do so well without it!—star-ing us in the face. That mother should have insanely *let* me, should so vulgarly have taken it for my natural, my social career—*that's* the disgusting, humiliating thing: with the lovely account it gives of

both of us!   But mother's view of a delicacy
in things!" she went on with scathing grimness; "mother's measure of anything, with
her grand 'gained cases' (there'll be another
yet, she finds them so easy!) of which she's
so publicly proud!   You see I've no margin,"
said Julia; letting him take it from her
flushed face as much as he would that her
mother hadn't left her an inch.   It was
that he should make use of the spade with
her for the restoration of a bit of a margin
just wide enough to perch on till the tide
of peril should have ebbed a little, it was
that he should give her *that* lift—!

Well, it was all there from him after these
last words; it was before her that he really
took hold.   "Oh, my dear child, I can see!
Of course there are people—ideas change
in our society so fast!—who are not in sympathy with the old American freedom and
who read, I dare say, all sorts of uncanny
things into it.   Naturally you must take
them as they are—from the moment," said
Murray Brush, who had lighted, by her leave,

a cigarette, "your life-path does, for weal
or for woe, cross with theirs." He had
every now and then such an elegant phrase.
"Awfully interesting, certainly, your case.
It's enough for me that it *is* yours—I make
it my own. I put myself absolutely in
your place; you'll understand from me,
without professions, won't you? that I do.
Command me in every way! What I do
like is the sympathy with which you've inspired *him*. I don't, I'm sorry to say, happen to know him personally"—he smoked
away, looking off; "but of course one knows
all about him generally, and I'm sure he's
right for you, I'm sure it would be charming,
if you yourself think so. Therefore trust
me and even—what shall I say?—leave it
to me a little, won't you?" He had been
watching, as in his fumes, the fine growth
of his possibilities; and with this he turned
on her the large warmth of his charity. It
was like a subscription of a half-a-million.
"I'll take care of you."

She found herself for a moment looking

up at him from as far below as the point
from which the school-child, with round
eyes raised to the wall, gazes at the parti-
colored map of the world. Yes, it was a
warmth, it was a special benignity, that
had never yet dropped on her from any one;
and she wouldn't for the first few moments
have known how to describe it or even
quite what to do with it. Then, as it still
rested, his fine improved expression aiding,
the sense of what had happened came over
her with a rush. She was being, yes, pat-
ronized; and that was really as new to her
—the freeborn American girl who might, if
she had wished, have got engaged and dis-
engaged not six times but sixty—as it would
have been to be crowned or crucified. The
Frenches themselves didn't do it — the
Frenches themselves didn't dare it. It was
as strange as one would: she recognized it
when it came, but anything might have come
rather—and it was coming by (of all people
in the world) Murray Brush! It over-
whelmed her; still she could speak, with

however faint a quaver and however sick a smile. "You'll lie for me like a gentle-man?"

"As far as that goes till I'm black in the face!" And then while he glowed at her and she wondered if he would pointedly look his lies that way, and if, in fine, his florid, gallant, knowing, almost winking intelligence, *common* as she had never seen the common vivified, would represent his notion of "blackness": "See here, Julia; I'll do more."

"'More'—?"

"Everything. I'll take it right in hand. I'll fling over you—"

"Fling over me—?" she continued to echo as he fascinatingly fixed her.

"Well, the biggest *kind* of rose-colored mantle!" And this time, oh, he did wink: it *would* be the way he was going to wink (and in the grandest good faith in the world) when indignantly denying, under inquisition, that there had been "a sign or a scrap" between them. But there was more to

come; he decided she should have it all.
"Julia, you've got to know now." He
hung fire but an instant more. "Julia, I'm
going to be married." His "Julias" were
somehow death to her; she could feel that
even *through* all the rest. "Julia, I an-
nounce my engagement."

"Oh, lordy, lordy!" she wailed: it might
have been addressed to Mr. Pitman.

The force of it had brought her to her feet,
but he sat there smiling up as at the natural
tribute of her interest. "I tell you before
any one else; it's not to be 'out' for a day or
two yet. But we want you to know; *she*
said that as soon as I mentioned to her that
I had heard from you. I mention to her
everything, you see!"—and he almost sim-
pered while, still in his seat, he held the end
of his cigarette, all delicately and as for a
form of gentle emphasis, with the tips of
his fine fingers. "You've not met her,
Mary Lindeck, I think: she tells me she
hasn't the pleasure of knowing you, but she
desires it so much—particularly longs for

it. She'll take an interest too," he went on;
"you must let me immediately bring her to
you. She has heard so much about you
and she really wants to see you."

"Oh mercy *me!*" poor Julia gasped again
—so strangely did history repeat itself and
so did this appear the echo, on Murray
Brush's lips, and quite to drollery, of that
sympathetic curiosity of Mrs. Drack's which
Mr. Pitman had, as they said, voiced. Well,
there had played before her the vision of a
ledge of safety in face of a rising tide; but
this deepened quickly to a sense more for-
lorn, the cold swish of waters already up to
her waist and that would soon be up to her
chin. It came really but from the air of her
friend, from the perfect benevolence and
high unconsciousness with which he kept
his posture—as if to show he could patronize her from below upward quite as well as
from above down. And as she took it all in,
as it spread to a flood, with the great lumps
and masses of truth it was floating, she
knew inevitable submission, not to say sub-

mersion, as she had never known it in her
life; going down and down before it, not
even putting out her hands to resist or cling
by the way, only reading into the young
man's very face an immense fatality and,
for all his bright nobleness, his absence of
rancor or of protesting pride, the great gray
blankness of her doom. It was as if the
earnest Miss Lindeck, tall and mild, high
and lean, with eye-glasses and a big nose,
but "marked" in a noticeable way, elegant
and distinguished and refined, as you could
see from a mile off, and as graceful, for common despair of imitation, as the curves of
the "copy" set of old by one's writing-master
—it was as if this stately well-wisher, whom
indeed she had never exchanged a word
with, but whom she had recognized and
placed and winced at as soon as he spoke of
her, figured there beside him now as also in
portentous charge of her case.

He had ushered her into it in that way,
as if his mere right word sufficed; and Julia
could see them throne together, beautifully

at one in all the interests they now shared, and regard her as an object of almost tender solicitude. It was positively as if they had become engaged for her good—in such a happy light as it shed. That was the way people you had known, known a bit intimately, looked at you as soon as they took on the high matrimonial propriety that sponged over the more or less wild past to which you belonged and of which, all of a sudden, they were aware only through some suggestion it made them for reminding you definitely that you still had a place. On her having had a day or two before to meet Mrs. Drack and to rise to her expectation she had seen and felt herself act, had above all admired herself, and had at any rate known what she said, even though losing, at her altitude, any distinctness in the others. She could have repeated later on the detail of her performance—if she hadn't preferred to keep it with her as a mere locked-up, a mere unhandled treasure. At present, however, as everything was for her at first

deadened and vague, true to the general
effect of sounds and motions in water, she
couldn't have said afterwards what words
she spoke, what face she showed, what impression she made—at least till she had
pulled herself round to precautions. She
only knew she had turned away, and that
this movement must have sooner or later
determined his rising to join her, his decid-
ing to accept it, gracefully and condoningly
—condoningly in respect to her natural
emotion, her inevitable little pang—for an
intimation that they would be better on
their feet.

They trod then afresh their ancient paths;
and though it pressed upon her hatefully
that he must have taken her abruptness for
a smothered shock, the flare-up of her old
feeling at the breath of his news, she had
still to see herself condemned to allow him
this, condemned really to encourage him
in the mistake of believing her suspicious
of feminine spite and doubtful of Miss Lindeck's zeal. She was so far from doubtful

[74]

that she was but too appalled at it and at
the officious mass in which it loomed, and
this instinct of dread, before their walk was
over, before she had guided him round to
one of the smaller gates, there to slip off
again by herself, was positively to find on
the bosom of her flood a plank by the aid
of which she kept in a manner and for the
time afloat. She took ten minutes to pant,
to blow gently, to paddle disguisedly, to
accommodate herself, in a word, to the ele-
ments she had let loose; but as a reward of
her effort at least she then saw how her determined vision accounted for everything.
Beside her friend on the bench she had truly
felt all his cables cut, truly swallowed down
the fact that if he still perceived she was
pretty—and *how* pretty!—it had ceased ap-
preciably to matter to him. It had lighted
the folly of her preliminary fear, the fear of
his even yet to some effect of confusion or
other inconvenience for her, proving more
alive to the quotable in her, as she had called
it, than to the inexpressible. She had reck-

[75]

oned with the awkwardness of that possible
failure of his measure of her charm, by
which his renewed apprehension of her
grosser ornaments, those with which he had
most affinity, might too much profit; but
she need have concerned herself as little for
his sensibility on one head as on the other.
She had ceased personally, ceased materi-
ally—in respect, as who should say, to any
optical or tactile advantage—to exist for
him, and the whole office of his manner had
been the more piously and gallantly to dress
the dead presence with flowers. This was
all to his credit and his honor, but what it
clearly certified was that their case was at
last not even one of spirit reaching out to
spirit. *He* had plenty of spirit—had all the
spirit required for his having engaged himself to Miss Lindeck, into which result, once
she had got her head well up again, she read,
as they proceeded, one sharp meaning after
another. It was therefore toward the subtler
essence of that mature young woman alone
that he was occupied in stretching; what

was definite to him about Julia Bride being merely, being entirely—which was indeed thereby quite enough—that she _might_ end by scaling her worldly height. They would push, they would shove, they would "boost," they would arch both their straight backs as pedestals for her tiptoe; and at the same time, by some sweet prodigy of mechanics, she would pull them up and up with her.

Wondrous things hovered before her in the course of this walk; her consciousness had become, by an extraordinary turn, a music-box in which, its lid well down, the most remarkable tunes were sounding. It played for her ear alone, and the lid, as she might have figured, was her firm plan of holding out till she got home, of not betraying —to her companion at least—the extent to which she was demoralized. To see him think her demoralized by mistrust of the sincerity of the service to be meddlesomely rendered her by his future wife— she would have hurled herself publicly into the lake there at their side, would have splashed, in her beautiful clothes, among the frightened swans, rather than invite him to that ineptitude. Oh, her sincerity, Mary Lindeck's—she would be drenched with her sincerity, and she would be drenched, yes, with *his;* so that, from inward convulsion to convulsion, she had, before they reached their gate, pulled up in the path. There was something her head had been full of these three or four minutes, the intensest little tune of the music-box, and it had made its way to her lips now; belonging—for all the good it could do her!—to the two or three sorts of solicitude she might properly express.

"I hope *she* has a fortune, if you don't mind my speaking of it: I mean some of the money we didn't in *our* time have—and that we missed, after all, in our poor way and for what we then wanted of it, so quite dreadfully."

She had been able to wreathe it in a grace quite equal to any he himself had employed; and it was to be said for him also that he

kept up, on this, the standard. "Oh, she's
not, thank goodness, at all badly off, poor
dear. We shall do very well. How sweet
of you to have thought of it! May I tell her
that too?" he splendidly glared. Yes, he
glared—how couldn't he, with what his
mind was really full of? But, all the same,
he came just here, by her vision, nearer than
at any other point to being a gentleman.
He came quite within an ace of it—with
his taking from her thus the prescription
of humility of service, his consenting to act
in the interest of her avidity, his letting her
mount that way, on his bowed shoulders, to
the success in which he could suppose she
still believed. He couldn't know, he would
never know, that she had then and there
ceased to believe in it—that she saw as clear
as the sun in the sky the exact manner in
which, between them, before they had done,
the Murray Brushes, all zeal and sincerity,
all interest in her interesting case, would
dish, would ruin, would utterly destroy her.
He wouldn't have needed to go on, for the

force and truth of this; but he did go on—
he was as crashingly consistent as a motor-
car without a brake. He was visibly in love
with the idea of what they might do for her
and of the rare "social" opportunity that
they would, by the same stroke, embrace.
How he had been offhand with it, how he
had made it parenthetic, that he didn't
happen "personally" to know Basil French
—as if it would have been at all likely he
should know him, even *im*personally, and
as if he could conceal from her the fact that,
since she had made him her overture, this
gentleman's name supremely baited her
hook! Oh, they would help Julia Bride if
they could—they would do their remarkable
best; but they would at any rate have made
his acquaintance over it, and she might indeed leave the rest to their thoroughness.
He would already have known, he would
already have heard; her appeal, she was
more and more sure, wouldn't have come
to him as a revelation. He had already
talked it over with *her*, with Miss Lindeck,

to whom the Frenches, in their fortress, had
never been accessible, and his whole attitude
bristled, to Julia's eyes, with the betrayal
of her hand, her voice, her pressure, her calculation. His tone in fact, as he talked,
fairly thrust these things into her face.
" But you must see her for yourself. You'll
judge her. You'll love her. My dear child "
—he brought it all out, and if he spoke of
children he might, in his candor, have been
himself infantine—" my dear child, she's the
person to do it for you. Make it over to
her; but," he laughed, " of course see her
first! Couldn't you," he wound up—for they
were now near their gate, where she was to
leave him—" couldn't you just simply make
us meet him, at tea say, informally; just *us*
alone, as pleasant old friends of whom you'd
have so naturally and frankly spoken to
him: and then see what we'd *make* of that?"

It was all in his expression; he couldn't
keep it out of that, and his shining good
looks couldn't: ah he was so fatally much
too handsome for her! So the gap showed

just there, in his admirable mask and his
admirable eagerness; the yawning little
chasm showed where the gentleman fell
short. But she took this in, she took everything in, she felt herself do it, she heard herself say, while they paused before separation
that she quite saw the point of the meeting,
as he suggested, at her tea. She would
propose it to Mr. French and would let
them know; and he must assuredly bring
Miss Lindeck, bring her "right away,"
bring her soon, bring *them*, his fiancée and
her, together somehow, and as quickly as
possible—so that they *should* be old friends
before the tea. She would propose it to Mr.
French, propose it to Mr. French: that
hummed in her ears as she went—after she
had really got away; hummed as if she were
repeating it over, giving it out to the passers,
to the pavement, to the sky, and all as in
wild discord with the intense little concert
of her music-box. The extraordinary thing
too was that she quite believed she should
do it, and fully meant to; desperately, fan-

SHE YIELDED TO THE BITTERNESS

tastically passive—since she almost reeled
with it as she proceeded—she was capable
of proposing anything to any one: capable
too of thinking it likely Mr. French would
come, for he had never on her previous pro-
posals declined anything. Yes, she would
keep it up to the end, this pretence of owing
them salvation, and might even live to take
comfort in having done for them what they
wanted. What they wanted *couldn't* but
be to get at the Frenches, and what Miss
Lindeck above all wanted, baffled of it other-
wise, with so many others of the baffled,
was to get at Mr. French—for all Mr. French
would want of either of them!—still more
than Murray did. It was not till after she
had got home, got straight into her own
room and flung herself on her face, that she
yielded to the full taste of the bitterness of
missing a connection, missing the man himself, with power to create such a social appetite, such a grab at what might be gained
by them. He could make people, even people like these two and whom there were still

[83]

other people to envy, he could make them push and snatch and scramble like that—and then remain as incapable of taking her from the hands of such patrons as of receiving her straight, say, from those of Mrs. Drack. It was a high note, too, of Julia's wonderful composition that, even in the long, lonely moan of her conviction of her now certain ruin, all this grim lucidity, the perfect clearance of passion, but made her supremely proud of him.

THE END